For Adrian & Roo

A Feiwel and Friends Book
An imprint of Macmillan Publishing, LLC
120 Broadway, New York, N.Y. 10271

Our books may be purchased in bulk for promotional, educational, or business use.
Please contact your local bookseller or the Macmillan Corporate and Premium Sales Department at
(800) 221-7945 ext. 5442 or by email at MacmillanSpecialMarkets@macmillan.com.

Library of Congress Control Number: 2019948799.
ISBN 978-1-250-31695-0

Book design by Laura Breen and Kathleen Breitenfeld

Some of the original artwork was created on paper using a black Sharpie marker,
then scanned into the computer and finished digitally using a Wacom tablet and pen.
All other drawings were digitally created solely using the Wacom tablet and pen in Photoshop.

Feiwel and Friends logo designed by Filomena Tuosto

First Edition, 2020

1 3 5 7 9 10 8 6 4 2

mackids.com

I See a Shadow

Laura Breen

FEIWEL AND FRIENDS
NEW YORK

Everything has a shadow.

Especially when the sun is bright.

Sometimes you can see a shadow even when it is night.

A tree's shadow can be long and tall.
Just like a tree, you see?

A cat's furry tail and pointy ears make its shadow unique.

Depending on the time of day

and where the sun is in the sky,

shadows will change shape,
place, and size.

A small person's shadow
will sometimes look tall . . .

. . . and a tall person's shadow
can look rather small.

Shadows can surprise us.

And sometimes look funny.

Best of all are the ones you make

when it's bright and sunny.

A shadow can be
as big as a building . . .

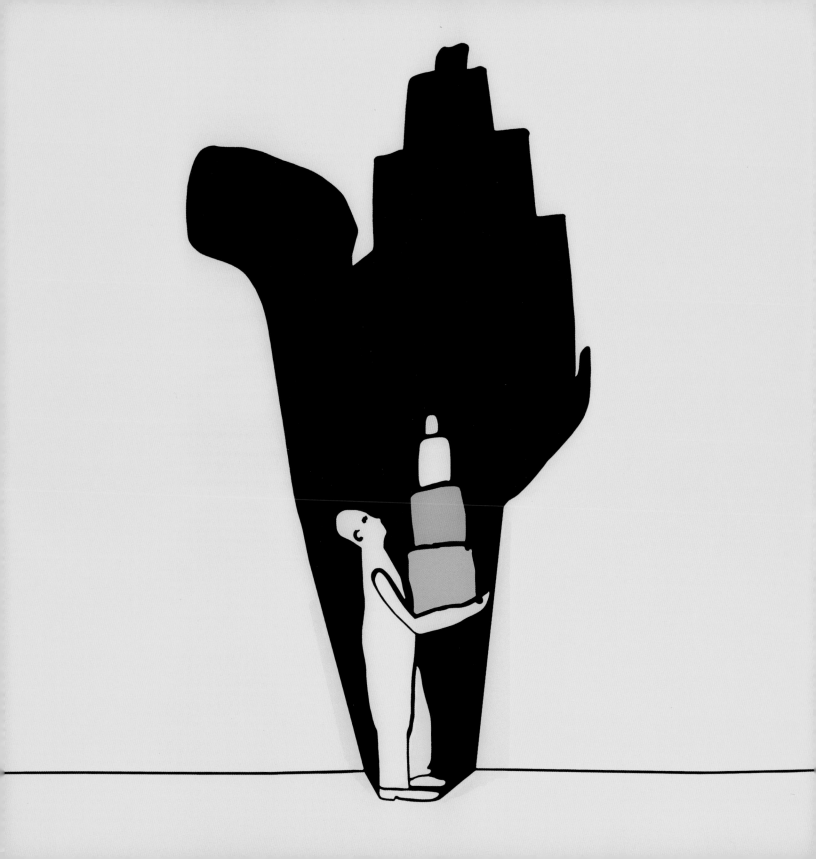

. . . or as small as a mouse.

See how many shadows you can
find around your house.